© 1995 Geddes & Grosset Ltd
Published by Geddes & Grosset Ltd,
New Lanark, Scotland.

ISBN 1 85534 563 3

Printed and bound in Great Britain.

The Wolf and the Seven Little Kids

Retold by Judy Hamilton
Illustrated by R. James Binnie

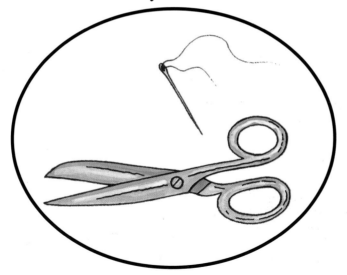

Tarantula Books

Once upon a time there was a mother goat who had seven little kids. She loved them dearly and tried to keep them safe. One day she had to go out into the forest for some food, so she gathered her children together to give them some instructions.

"Lock the doors and windows after I have gone," she told them, "and do not let anybody come in. There is a big wolf in the forest who would eat you all for his dinner if he could. If he does come to the house he may come in disguise, but you will always be able to tell him from his growling voice and his black feet."

The kids listened carefully and when their mother left, they locked all the doors behind her.

Their mother had not been gone long when there was a knock at the door and a voice called:

"Open the door, my dears! It is I, your mother. I have a lovely surprise for you all!"

But the seven kids heard the growling in the caller's voice and recognized the wolf.

"You are not our mother. She has a soft voice, and you are growling! You are the wolf!"

The wolf was angry that he had been recognized. He went and bought some chalk which he swallowed to make his voice softer. Then he went back to the cottage and knocked on the door again, calling gently:

"Open the door, my dears! It is I, your mother. I have a lovely surprise for you!"

But the wolf foolishly put his paws up on the windowsill to try to see the seven kids. The kids recognized his black hairy feet at once.

"You are not our mother!" they called. "You have black feet, but our mother has white feet. You are the wolf. Go away!"

The wolf was very angry, but would not give up. He ran to the mill and called to the miller:

"I have got sore feet. Please rub some dough on them for me!"

The miller was frightened of the wolf and did as he was asked. Then the wolf said:

"Now give me some flour to dip my feet in."

The miller guessed that the wolf was trying to trick somebody, but he dared not refuse.

The wolf went back to the cottage and knocked on the door for a third time:

"Open the door, my dears! It is I, your mother. I have a lovely surprise for you!"

The seven little kids were still suspicious.

"Put you feet up on the windowsill so that we can look at them!"

The wolf put his feet up on the windowsill. The kids saw the feet, whitened with flour, and they had heard the voice, softened with chalk. They did not recognize the wolf. They thought that it really was their mother, back from the forest. And so they opened the door. How frightened they were to see the wolf standing on the doorstep!

They ran in all directions, trying to hide.

The first little kid dived underneath the table, the second jumped into bed, the third hid inside the stove, the fourth ran into the kitchen, the fifth shut himself in a cupboard and the sixth crawled under a big washing bowl. The seventh and youngest could see nowhere else to hide except inside the case of the grandfather clock.

Poor little kids! One by one, the wolf found them. One by one, he swallowed them whole. He swallowed the first, the second, the third, the fourth, the fifth and then the sixth little kid. After that, he could not find any more and so he left. Only the seventh little kid was saved, hiding in the grandfather clock. There he stayed until his mother came home from the forest.

The mother goat came home to a terrible mess. Tables and chairs were overturned, beds were torn apart and broken china covered the floor. Where were her dear children? She called out their names but could hear nothing. So she stood in the middle of the floor and wept, thinking that they had all gone. Then she heard a muffled voice coming from the grandfather clock:

"I'm in here, mother!"

She opened the clock case and let the youngest kid out. He told his poor mother that the wolf had eaten all the other kids. The mother goat was most dreadfully upset. She could not bear to stay in the house where her children had been eaten. She left, taking the seventh little kid with her.

The wolf had swallowed the six little kids far too quickly. And six kids, all at once, was far too much to eat. Not long after he left the cottage, his stomach began to churn. He felt very heavy and uncomfortable. He decided to rest for a short while under a tree before he continued his journey back to his den at the other side of the forest. He lay down, groaning from the weight of the six little kids inside his stomach. Within a very short time, the wolf had fallen fast asleep.

And so it was that soon after the mother goat and the seventh little kid had left the cottage, they found the wolf lying sleeping there. They tiptoed up to take a closer look at him.

Suddenly, the mother goat noticed that the wolf's stomach was moving. Something was struggling inside. Could the six kids still possibly be alive? The mother goat turned to the youngest kid and whispered quietly, so as not to wake the wolf:

"Quickly, my dear, run home and find my biggest scissors, a needle and some strong thread. Then bring them back to me as fast as you can. We have to hurry, before the wolf wakes up, or he will catch us and eat us too."

The seventh little kid ran home as fast as his legs would carry him and was soon back at his mother's side. He handed her the scissors, the needle and the thread and she set to work at once.

As the wolf lay there snoring, the mother goat carefully began to cut open his stomach with the scissors. She had hardly made the first snip when she saw the head of the first little kid come popping out. He was still alive. The mother goat carried on cutting into the wolf's stomach and soon the second little kid popped out. After that came the third little kid and then the fourth, the fifth and then finally the sixth. The mother goat counted all her children again and again. They were all alive and well!

The little kids wanted to jump and shout for joy, but their mother signalled them to hush.

"The celebrations must come later," she whispered. "We still have work to do!"

The seven little kids listened carefully to their mother.

"Go and fetch as many big stones from the river as you can," she said, "and bring them back to me. We must fill this beast's stomach!"

The seven little kids set off to do as their mother asked as quickly and as quietly as they could. They ran to the river and heaved and pushed some of the biggest stones that they could see out of the water. Then they pushed and rolled them over to where their mother waited. One by one, the mother goat lifted the heavy stones into the open stomach of the still sleeping wolf. Then she sent the seven little kids back to the river to get some more.

When the second load of stones had been stuffed into the wolf's stomach, it was bulging fit to burst.

"That should be enough now," said the mother goat to her children. "You can rest now while I finish off this little job."

So saying, she took the needle and thread and began to sew up the wolf's stomach with neat, strong stitches. How strange it looked when she had finished! It was all lumpy and bumpy and bulging all over. The mother goat turned to her children once more.

"Now we must hide," she said, "and wait until the wolf wakes up."

A short while later the wolf woke up feeling thirsty and tried to get to his feet. The stones rattled inside his bulging stomach.

"I feel as if I have eaten a pile of stones instead of six little kids!" he groaned.

The goat family, hiding close by, watched the wolf stagger to the river to get some water. The heavy stones rattling inside him made every step painful. When the wolf reached the river, he leaned over to take a drink, but the weight of the stones in his stomach made him topple over. He sank to the bottom of the river and drowned.

"Now," the mother goat said to her seven dear children, "We can go home and celebrate. We are safe from the wolf forever!"